NOV- - 2018

❧ MY NOTE FOR YOU ❧

Watching my daughter, Mae, I am filled with such an ache
for the love I have for her (as I'm sure every parent feels
watching her child). I think about how much we can lose —
how much fire in the belly can fade out — as we grow up.
It's easy to forget to take time to just . . . be.

I want young girls and women to feel empowered, inspired,
free to be themselves. I want everyone to find joy in the
"little" things. It's okay to act silly; it's okay to feel sad.
It's important to be brave, but it's okay to be scared.
Be curious. Be strong. Be vulnerable. I want girls to live life
on their own terms. To never be afraid of loving oneself —
flaws and all — in a world that demands perfection.

My daughter has taught me so much that I had
forgotten, and, in some cases, things that no one thought
to teach me as a child. And I want to pass this on to
all the girls out there. My wish for you all is that no
matter who you are, you are enough.

Kathryn Shelton

To the good women at Lenny Letter for inspiring
me to write this in the first place.

And to Mae Marie and her big brother, Leonard Henry.
I am most proud of being your Mama. And Ethan, for it all.
— K.H.

For Rowan: Always be yourself!
— Brigette Barrager

Text copyright © 2018 by Kathryn Hahn
Illustrations copyright © 2018 by Brigette Barrager

Library of Congress Cataloging-in-Publication number 2017021221

ISBN 978-1-338-15040-7
10 9 8 7 6 5 4 3 2 1   18 19 20 21 22

Printed in China 38
First edition, October 2018
The artwork for this book was created with
custom painterly brushes in Adobe Photoshop.
The text type was set in Halewyn.
Hand lettering by Angela Southern
Book design by Sunny Lee

words by **KATHRYN HAHN**   pictures by **BRIGETTE BARRAGER**

My Wish
for You

Orchard Books
An Imprint of Scholastic Inc.
New York

My wishes for you are many.
But at the top of the wishes:
I want YOU to be YOU.

And wherever you go, I hope you will always remember the **you** that you are right now. The **you** that knows to...

SING all the time. NAP whenever.

DRAW
cat whiskers on your face.

Dress up.
Play PRETEND
with fancy shoes.

Eat all the Yummies.

Love your big beautiful belly.

Love
your whole
beautiful
self!

Sit on the floor of a shower and Pretend you are in a rainstorm.

Take long, long baths.

Look for that "sparkle."

Catch as many as you can!

Be afraid. Be FEARLESS.

Have BIG, BIG feelings.

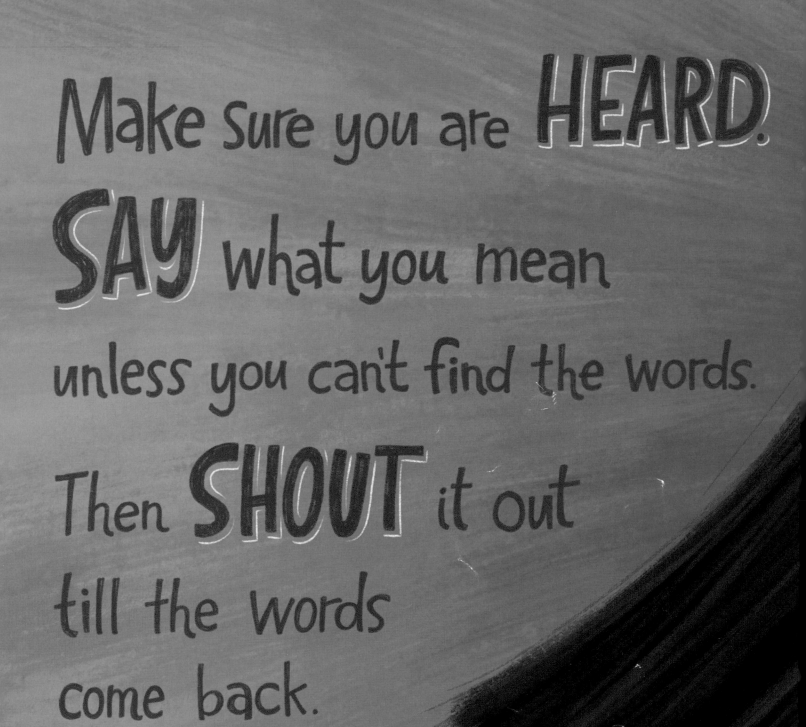

Make sure you are **HEARD.**
SAY what you mean
unless you can't find the words.

Then **SHOUT** it out
till the words
come back.

Don't give yourself away.

Protect your HEART.

Let people **EARN** the right
to be your friend.

Don't care at all if not
everyone likes you.
Find your band.
And get dirty with them.

Know everything
and nothing.

TREES

BUGS

FIELD GUIDE

flowers

Go deep, deep, deep.
Be curious.

Embrace your shyness.

Be
alone
in your
room.
Take time for you.

Ask for that **KISS** if you want it.
Ask for that **CUDDLE** when you need it.

Ask for what you need.

"Can we listen to that song where we both want to cry with no tears?"

Let yourself fall...

...Then pick yourself **UP**.

My wish is that you remember to dream, my sweet. You are all you need to make your wishes come true.

Because you are the only YOU.